TRAIN SONG

by *Diane Siebert*

paintings by Mike Wimmer

HarperCollins*Publishers*

Train Song

Text copyright © 1981 by Diane Siebert
Illustrations copyright © 1990 by Michael L. Wimmer
The poem "Train Song" was first published in *Cricket* magazine in 1981.
Printed in Mexico. All rights reserved.
Typography by Al Cetta

Library of Congress Cataloging-in-Publication Data
Siebert, Diane.
Train song / by Diane Siebert ; illustrated by Mike Wimmer. — 1st ed.
p. cm.
Summary: Rhymed text and illustrations describe the journeys of a
variety of transcontinental trains.
ISBN 0-690-04726-6. — ISBN 0-690-04728-2 (lib. bdg.)
ISBN 0-06-443340-4 (pbk.)
[1. Railroads—Trains—Fiction. 2. Stories in rhyme.] 1. Wimmer,
Mike, ill. II. Title.
PZ8.3.S5725Tp 1990   88-389
[E]—dc19   CIP
                                                      AC

out in back
railroad track
clickety-clack
clickety-clack

locomotives
cars in tow

going places:
Buffalo
New York City
Boston, Mass.
slowing 'neath the overpass
Dallas
Fort Worth
Abilene
with stops at all points
in between

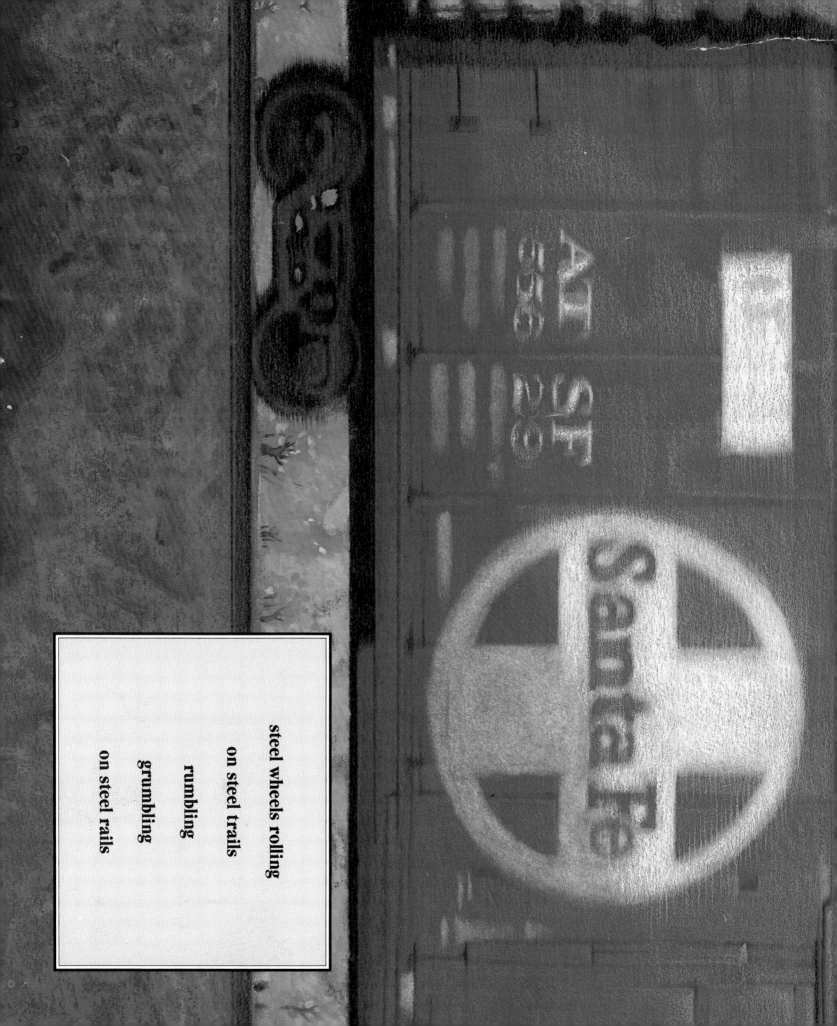

steel wheels rolling
on steel trails
rumbling
grumbling
on steel rails

engineers with striped hats
head-of-the-line aristocrats
up in front
sitting high
see them wave as they go by

great trains

freight trains

talk about your late trains

the 509

right on time

straight through to L. A.

whistle blows

there she goes

slicing through the day

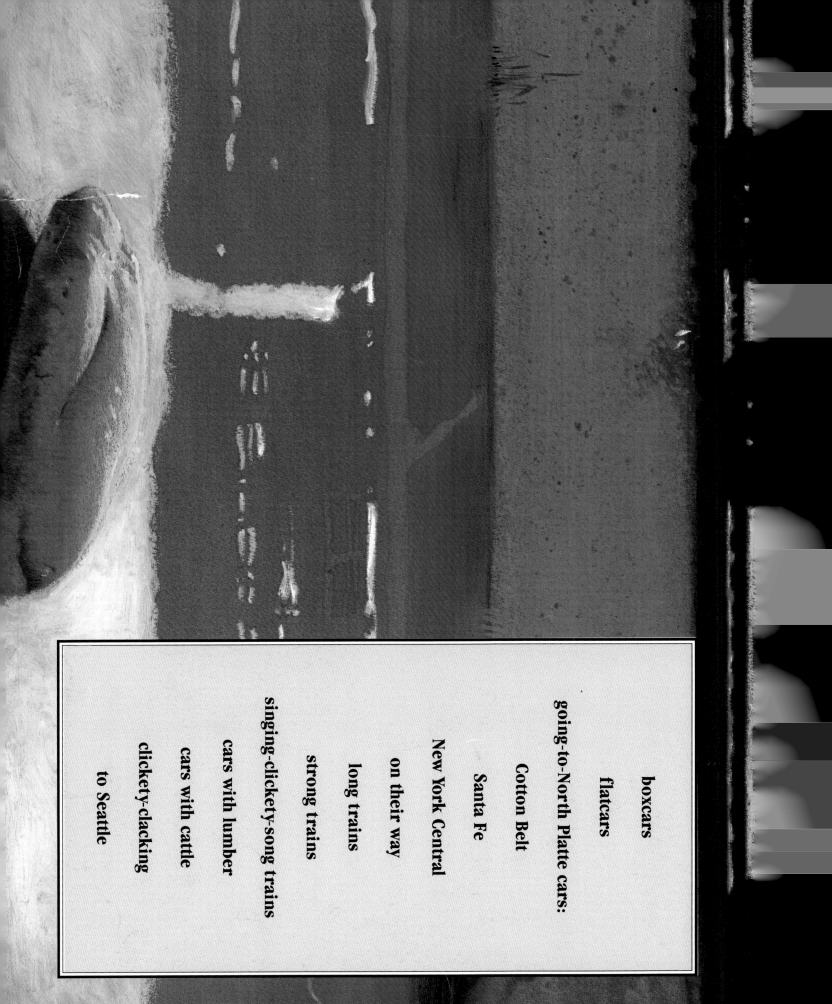

boxcars

flatcars

going-to-North Platte cars:

Cotton Belt

Santa Fe

New York Central

on their way

long trains

strong trains

singing-clickety-song trains

cars with lumber

cars with cattle

clickety-clacking

to Seattle

cars piled high with automobiles

wheels

on

wheels

on

wheels

on

wheels

tank cars hauling gasoline

diesel oil and kerosene

thirty hoppers in a row

hauling spuds from Idaho

caboose of yellow at the end

disappearing 'round the bend

trains with passengers on board

clickety-clacking

rolling toward

their destinations far away

clickety-clacking

night and day

coaches

club cars

diners, too

dome cars with a perfect view

signal lights

green

yellow

red

railroad station up ahead

rolling
rolling
into town
toward the platform
slowing down
creaking
clanking
air brakes squeal
moaning
groaning
steel on steel

PASSENGER TRAIN SCHEDULE

TRACK	TRAIN NAME	DEPARTS	ARRIVES
4	Walla Walla	2:30	9:30a
8	Bay Area Sleeper	3:00	12
3	Durango	6:00	

Overnighter to the bay
arrive at noon on Saturday
get a sleeper
don't be late
she's waiting on Track number 8

head conductor
dressed in black
peering up and down the track
checks his watch
now hear him shout:
"ALL ABOARD"
she's pulling out!

through the tunnel

going fast

clickety-clack

she's roaring past

the cities, suburbs, little towns

past forest greens and desert browns

spikes and crossties
smooth, worn rails
through the twilight
whistle wails
feel the rhythm
hear the sound
clickety-clacking
homeward bound

say good night

and

wave good-bye

hear the railroad lullaby